MY SPECIAL ONE AND ONLY

Joe Berger

Dial Books for Young Readers
an imprint of Penguin Group (USA) Inc.

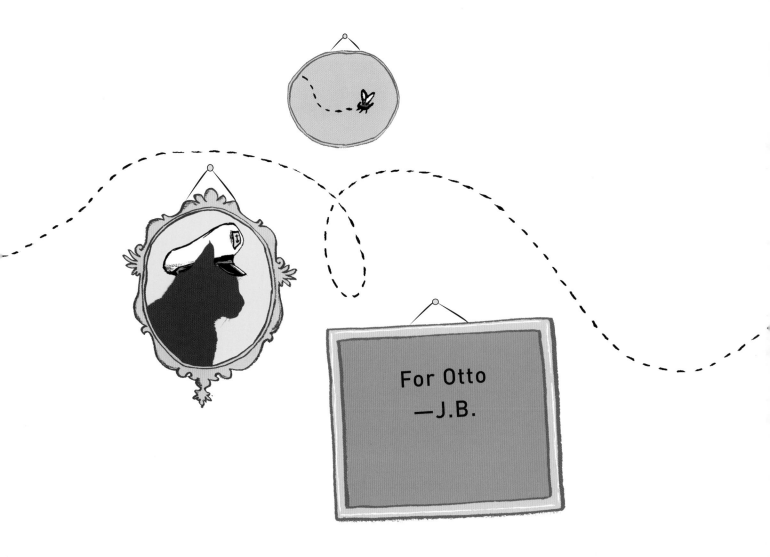

For Otto
—J.B.

DIAL BOOKS FOR YOUNG READERS A division of Penguin Young Readers Group
Published by The Penguin Group • Penguin Group (USA) Inc., 375 Hudson Street, New York, NY 10014, U.S.A. • Penguin Group (Canada), 90 Eglinton
Avenue East, Suite 700, Toronto, Ontario, Canada M4P 2Y3 (a division of Pearson Penguin Canada Inc.) •Penguin Books Ltd, 80 Strand, London WC2R
0RL, England • Penguin Ireland, 25 St. Stephen's Green, Dublin 2, Ireland (a division of Penguin Books Ltd) • Penguin Group (Australia), 250 Camberwell
Road, Camberwell, Victoria 3124, Australia (a division of Pearson Australia Group Pty Ltd) • Penguin Books India Pvt Ltd, 11 Community Centre,
Panchsheel Park, New Delhi - 110 017, India • Penguin Group (NZ), 67 Apollo Drive, Rosedale, Auckland 0632, New Zealand (a division of Pearson New
Zealand Ltd) • Penguin Books (South Africa) (Pty) Ltd, 24 Sturdee Avenue, Rosebank, Johannesburg 2196, South Africa • Penguin Books Ltd, Registered
Offices: 80 Strand, London WC2R 0RL, England

First published in the United States 2012 by Dial Books for Young Readers
Published in the United Kingdom 2010 by Puffin Books under the title Bridget Fidget: Hold on Tight!
Copyright © 2010 by Joe Berger

10 9 8 7 6 5 4 3 2 1

Library of Congress Cataloging-in-Publication Data is available upon request.

When **Bridget Fidget's** wiggly tooth fell out,
she popped it under her pillow and told her favorite toy,
Captain Cat, to look out for tooth fairies.

Bridget's pet ladybug, Thunderhooves (not the tooth fairy)

Captain Cat was Bridget's ***special one and only***
and even in her dreams she held on tight to him.

The next morning, the tooth had gone
and in its place was a

SHINY GOLDEN COIN!

"Hold on tight to my shiny golden coin, Captain Cat," said Bridget.

"We're going shopping at the best store in the whole world."

HOP!

SKIP!

BOUNCE!

Bridget was so excited, she didn't wait for Mommy.
She SPIZZOOMED through the revolving doors
and headed straight for her favorite
part of the shop.

"Hold on tight, Captain Cat!"

SPIZZOOOOM!!

"Have you ever seen so many toy cats?" said Bridget to Captain Cat. "Of course, none of them are nearly as special as you!"

YIKES! NOW LOOK!

Just then Billy from school pedaled past in
his brand-new **Superzoom 500**.

"Hello, Bridget," said Billy. "Where's Captain Cat?"

"In my backpack, of course," replied Bridget,
turning around so Billy could see.

"No he isn't," said Billy.

And Billy was right. Captain Cat was
100% NOT THERE!!!

"Nooooooo!" cried Bridget.
"He's my *special one and only* and I've just got to find him!"

Bridget ran to tell Mommy . . .

but **tri*p*ped** . . .

and then *skidded*
through a pile of
cardboard boxes.

KABOOF!

When Bridget opened her eyes, everything looked very different and she was all alone.

But Bridget didn't
waste any time.
Quick as a flash,
she leaped to her feet.

"Hold on tight,
Captain Cat,"
she cried.

"I'm coming!"

But Bridget couldn't find Captain Cat ANYWHERE, so she sat down on a pink cloud and had some "quiet time."

"There you are, Bridget Fidget," said Billy.
"What are you doing in the window display?
Your mommy's looking for you."

"And I've looked everywhere for
Captain Cat," sobbed Bridget.
"He's my *special one and only*
and now he's **lost forever**
and I can't go on without him."

"Wait a minute,"
said Billy . . .

"Then there's only one thing to do," said Billy . . .

"HOLD ON TIGHT,

Bridget and Billy caught up with Captain Cat . . .

SCREEEEEEECH!

Everyone, that is,

except the little girl

named Marley who'd found

Captain Cat in her basket

and decided to take

care of him.

Luckily, Bridget had a bright idea. "Do you still have my shiny golden coin, Captain Cat?"

And with a bit of extra money from Mommy, Bridget knew just what to buy with it.

A
Ballet Cat
for Marley.

A
Racing Cat
for Billy . . .

And for Bridget and Captain Cat— "I GOT LOST IN **DINGLE BANG'S**" buttons.

"Oh, Captain Cat!
I'll **never** let
go of you again!"
said Bridget.
And she didn't.

All the way home . . .

all through supper . . .

even all the way through bath-time,
Bridget Fidget held on tight to Captain Cat.
"You're worth more than all the
shiny golden coins in the world," said Bridget.

"Besides, I'm not sure . . .
but I think I might have another wiggly tooth."